Four Stories
for Four Seasons

Prentice-Hall Inc.

ENGLEWOOD CLIFFS / NEW JERSEY

FOUR STORIES
❀ for ❀
FOUR SEASONS

stories and pictures by
Tomie de Paola

Prentice-Hall International, Inc., London
Prentice-Hall of Australia, Pty. Ltd., North Sydney
Prentice-Hall of Canada, Ltd., Toronto
Prentice-Hall of India Private Ltd., New Delhi
Prentice-Hall of Japan, Inc., Tokyo
Prentice-Hall of Southeast Asia Pte, Ltd., Singapore
10 9 8 7 6 5 4 3 2

Library of Congress Cataloging in Publication Data

De Paola, Thomas Anthony.
□ Four stories for four seasons.

□ SUMMARY: Four friends, a cat, dog, pig,
and frog, share the delights of each season.
□ [1. Seasons—Fiction. 2. Friendship—Fiction.
3. Animals—Fiction] I. Title.
PZ7.D439Fo   [E]   76-8837
ISBN 0-13-330175-3
          0-13-330100-1 (pbk.)

FOR MY FOUR FRIENDS · TRINA · DILYS · BART & JIM ·

SPRING

One fine spring day, Master Dog and
Missy Cat decided to ask Mistress Pig and
Mister Frog to join them in a stroll
through the park.

"What lovely crocuses and daffodils,"
said Missy Cat.

"I like the tulips, too,"said Master Dog.

"Nothing like a nice walk to make you
feel chipper," said Mister Frog.

"Oh, look! An ice cream stand,"
said Mistress Pig.

"I say," said Mister Frog,
"how about a row around the lake?"
"Let's do it!" said Master Dog.
"I've never been rowing before,"
said Missy Cat.
"Oh, you'll love it, Kitty,"
said Mistress Pig.

"Oh, we sail the ocean blue,"
sang Mister Frog.
"My balloon," squealed Mistress Pig.

"Oh dear," said Missy Cat.

"That's the first time *that's* ever
happened," said Master Dog.
"So sorry," muttered Mister Frog.
"Are you all right, Kitty dear?"
asked Mistress Pig.

"Rowing is so much fun!" said Missy Cat.
"When can we do it again?"

One day in early, early summer,
the four friends thought it would be fun
for each one to plant a garden.

They all worked very hard as the summer went by.

"Now that summer's almost over, my friends," said Mister Frog, "I think we should visit each other's gardens."

"We can have a Garden Viewing Day," said Missy Cat.

"Oh, goody," said Mistress Pig.

"Let's do it Thursday," said Master Dog.

The four friends agreed that Thursday would be a perfect day.

They all met at Missy Cat's garden.
"Pretty!" said Master Dog.
"Nothing like a well-planned
flower garden," said Mister Frog.
"Those marigolds look good enough
to eat," added Mistress Pig.
"Thank you, my dears,"
purred Missy Cat.

Next they went to Mister Frog's garden.
"Why, you have a water-lily and cattail
garden," said Master Dog.
"So original!" said Missy Cat.
"You must tell me your secret,"
whispered Mistress Pig.
"The secret is water," answered Mister Frog.
"Does look rather nice, doesn't it?" he added.

Mistress Pig's garden was next.
"Oh, Piggy sweet, how practical,"
said Missy Cat.
"Never have seen such pumpkins!"
said Mister Frog.
"And those carrots. I love carrots,"
said Master Dog.
"I'm so pleased you like it," said
Mistress Pig. "Here, taste these tomatoes.
They're delicious."

Finally they arrived at Master Dog's garden.

The three friends looked and looked.

"I say, Doggy—what happened?" asked Mister Frog.

"Poor Doggy, I'm *so* sorry for you," said Missy Cat.

"A *dirt* garden?" gasped Mistress Pig.

"You don't understand, dear friends,"
said Master Dog.

"It's a bone garden!"

FALL

One crisp fall day, Mistress Pig invited
her three friends to a dinner party.

"Let's sit here on the porch and look at
the beautiful fall colors," said Mistress Pig
when her friends arrived.

"Won't you have a little punch?"
she asked.

"You know, Piggy sweet, this is my
favorite time of the year," said Missy Cat.

"Mine too, Kitty dear," said Mistress Pig.

"That's why I wanted all of us to have
a lovely dinner together."

"Now, everyone sit down. I'm going out to the kitchen to put the finishing touches on the cucumber soup, the corn fritters and the turnip soufflé."

The three friends sat.

They waited.

And waited.

And waited.

"I wonder what's keeping Piggy?
I'm hungry," growled Master Dog.
"Let's go see," said Missy Cat.

"Oh, Piggy!" said the three friends.
"I started tasting the soup, the fritters,
the souffle and everything else to make
sure they were all right—and I just
couldn't stop," said Mistress Pig.
"Now I've ruined our dinner party."

"Oh, Piggy dear, don't cry.
We understand," said Missy Cat.
   "No problem, no problem at all,"
said Mister Frog.
   "Everybody—get your hats,"
said Master Dog.

"And for dessert, I think I'll have the chocolate mousse," said Mistress Pig to the waiter.

WINTER

Mister Frog always slept right through
the winter. Most frogs do.

But, even though he had a nice long rest
and didn't have to bother with the snow
and cold, he always missed Christmas.

His three friends told him how wonderful it was to celebrate the happy holiday.

"Oh, Froggy, you would love it! Turkey, plum pudding, candy canes, lots of good things to eat," said Mistress Pig.

"Candles, angels and Christmas trees," said Missy Cat.

"Yule logs, Christmas carols and Santa Claus," added Master Dog.

So Mister Frog decided to stay up and celebrate Christmas, too. He kept awake all through November.

By December first, Mister Frog was
busy making Christmas lists, planning a
Christmas dinner menu, writing out
his Christmas cards and thinking about
how he would decorate his house with holly
and greens.

But all of this made him very tired.
"I think I'll just take a tiny nap," he said.

Ding, dong, ding, dong, ding, dong,
the church bells rang out.
"Goodness," croaked Mister Frog,
"hope I haven't overslept."

But he had.
There were no turkeys left, no cranberries,
no candy canes, no Christmas wreaths.
In fact, all the stores were closed.
Mister Frog couldn't even find a
Christmas tree. And it was Christmas Eve.

Poor Froggy!

The doorbell rang ding-a-ling and Mister
Frog went to see who was at the door.
  "Ho, ho, ho, merry Christmas,"
said Santa Claus.

Ding-a-ling.
"Ho, ho, ho, merry Christmas,"
said Santa Claus.

Ding-a-ling.
"Ho, ho, ho, merry Christmas,"
said Santa Claus.

"Merry Christmas, merry Christmas, merry Christmas," said Mister Frog.

"Now let's hang up our stockings," said Master Dog.

"Here's the plum pudding!" said Mistress Pig.

"And we four friends are all celebrating Christmas together," said Missy Cat.

"Silent Night, Holy Night,
  All is calm, all is bright . . ."
sang the four friends.